JE WELLS
Wells, Rosemary.
Play with Max and Ruby /

Put Beginning Readers on the Right Track with
ALL ABOARD READING™

The All Aboard Reading series is especially designed for beginning readers. Written by noted authors and illustrated in full color, these are books that children really want to read—books to excite their imagination, expand their interests, make them laugh, and support their feelings. With fiction and nonfiction stories that are high interest and curriculum-related, All Aboard Reading books offer something for every young reader. And with four different reading levels, the All Aboard Reading series lets you choose which books are most appropriate for your children and their growing abilities.

Picture Readers
Picture Readers have super-simple texts, with many nouns appearing as rebus pictures. At the end of each book are 24 flash cards—on one side is a rebus picture; on the other side is the written-out word.

Station Stop 1
Station Stop 1 books are best for children who have just begun to read. Simple words and big type make these early reading experiences more comfortable. Picture clues help children to figure out the words on the page. Lots of repetition throughout the text helps children to predict the next word or phrase—an essential step in developing word recognition.

Station Stop 2
Station Stop 2 books are written specifically for children who are reading with help. Short sentences make it easier for early readers to understand what they are reading. Simple plots and simple dialogue help children with reading comprehension.

Station Stop 3
Station Stop 3 books are perfect for children who are reading alone. With longer text and harder words, these books appeal to children who have mastered basic reading skills. More complex stories captivate children who are ready for more challenging books.

In addition to All Aboard Reading books, look for All Aboard Math Readers™ (fiction stories that teach math concepts children are learning in school) and All Aboard Science Readers™ (nonfiction books that explore the most fascinating science topics in age-appropriate language).

All Aboard for happy reading!

Portions previously published in MAX'S TOYS, 1998, 1979 and BUNNY PARTY, 2001.

Library of Congress Control Number: 2002106372

ISBN 978-0-448-42854-3   E F G H I J

PLAY WITH MAX AND RUBY

Based on the characters of
ROSEMARY WELLS

Grosset & Dunlap • New York

 loved

Ruby's  Emily

so much.

"Max,"

said his sister,  ,

"Emily is 1 thing

you may not have."

 had a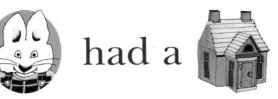

with chimneys,

but he still wanted

Emily.

"Max, you have

3

and 4 ,"

said .

"Stop looking at

Emily."

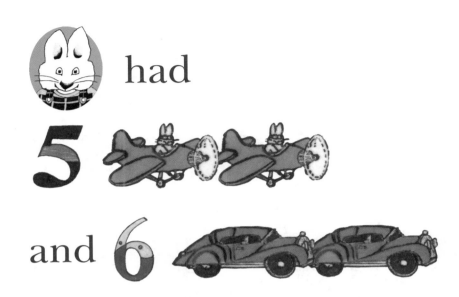 had

5 and **6** .

He had **7**

and a

with **8** legs.

But he still wanted

Emily.

"Go away, Max,"

said .

All 9 of Max's

fell down.

"Quiet," said ,

"Emily is asleep."

had a **1-0** car

 accident.

"Max,"

said  .

"I'll trade you

Emily for ALL

of your  ."